Ninarphay Tales

VOL I - IV

Leon Lowe

AuthorHouse™ UK
1663 Liberty Drive
Bloomington, IN 47403 USA
www.authorhouse.co.uk
UK TFN: 0800 0148641 (Toll Free inside the UK)
UK Local: 02036 956322 (+44 20 3695 6322 from outside the UK)

Because of the dynamic nature of the Internet, any web addresses or links contained
in this book may have changed since publication and may no longer be valid. The views
expressed in this work are solely those of the author and do not necessarily reflect the
views of the publisher, and the publisher hereby disclaims any responsibility for them.

Any people depicted in stock imagery provided by Getty Images are models,
and such images are being used for illustrative purposes only.
Certain stock imagery © Getty Images.

This book is printed on acid-free paper.

ISBN: 979-8-8230-8314-0 (sc)
ISBN: 979-8-8230-8313-3 (e)

Print information available on the last page.

Published by AuthorHouse 06/07/2023

authorHOUSE®

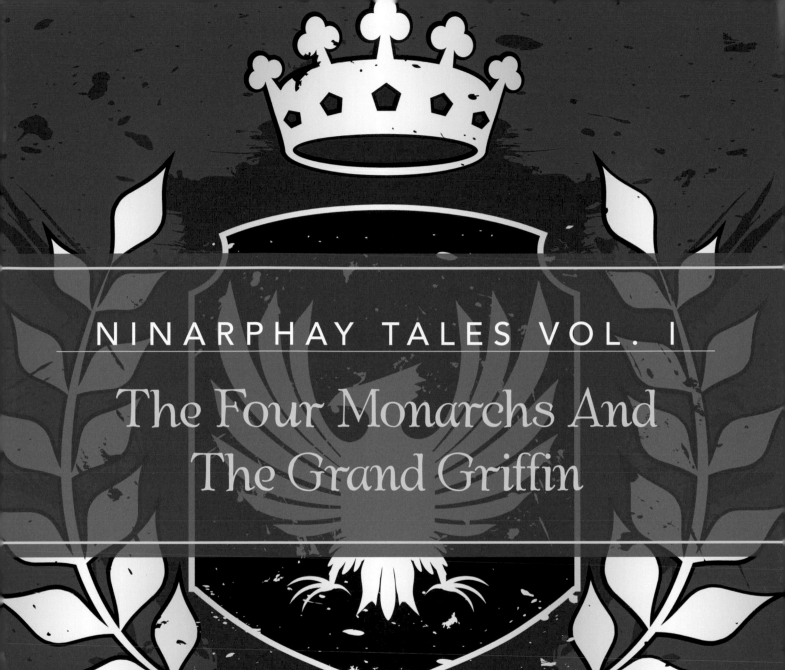

NINARPHAY TALES VOL. I

The Four Monarchs And
The Grand Griffin

Escape To Ninarphay

Four Young Women and a Great mythical Beast run from the Ruins of a Temple, and a Giant Ogre with a massive chopping Blade runs behind them shouting. The Griffin chants. "Free I raw an open Door releases the young from Transzalore." A great flash appears, and the four Young Women appear in a Forest.

Tresel, the lightest-looking one, says, "Where are we"? The Grand Griffin, without distress, tells them. We have escaped the World of Transzalore you were born to and have been promoted to the Contented Lands of Ninarphay. This is Ninarphay Forest." It is Night, and the four Desperate Women are in a Forest that is the Gateway from another Realm and leads into a Kingdom called Ninarphay, built by, Dwarves, Fairies, Elves and Banshees.

At the Gateway are four Women and a Grand Griffin; they are carrying Swords and panting their breath heavily.

Nivea is a Lady with Long hair and a Strong, Wise voice. She says to the Grand Griffin, "Grand Griffin, we have escaped the Temple of remorse and journeyed nearly our whole lives with you; what is next?"

Stin is the most Muscular of them, saying to the Group, "We have come a long way, Nivea; the Grand Griffin has been a kind and gentle guide. Please be patient with him." Giant-like, his wisdom is known through the ages and the Lands of Ninarphay. He tells them, "We have made it out of the Realm of Transzalore and are now in the Contented Realm of Ninarphay; here, your Destiny awaits you."

Tresel is the most attractive of them and also Sympathetic. She says, "We have done as your bidding Grand Griffin so what is next?"

The Grand Griffin, with a still and gentle tone, expresses to them, "It was me who was chosen as your Guide; therefore, it is me who will Award you your Entitlements".

The Grand Griffin extends his Talons and says, "This is my Righteous and Perfect Talon. Everything you need rests on my Fingertips; extend your arms towards me and embrace your Heart's Desire."

Nivea extends her Arms forward and places her hand on the Grand Griffins Talon. Her Palm catches into Fire, a magical glow of Red and Orange, and a Sword appears.

The Grand Griffin tells Nivea, "Nivea go to the East, and there you will Rule as the Eastern Monarch of the Sword and remember to Rule in the ways of Justice and Graciousness".

Nivea stands to the side of the Griffin and watches the others.

Tresel steps forward and places her hand on the Talon of the Grand Griffin. Tresels'sTress hand turns to Ice, her Hand magically Frosts into a Blue solid ember and a Pair of Sandals become apparent. She quickly removes her Hand.

The Grand Griffin wastes no time telling Tresel, "Tresel, you are the Monarch of the North; you will stand high in esteem and warm in the soul. Take this Gift and Rule in the Northern Kingdom with Justice and Graciousness."

Tresel steps back and witnesses the other Regents. Stin then steps forward she places her hand on the Talon of the Grand Griffin. Her Hand turns to Wood, a creaking noise, and Brown Bark magically ascends onto the Talon of the Griffin; she removes her Hand and an Escutcheon marked with the Symbol of the Griffin and two Crowns appear on the Escutcheon.

Stin says to the Grand Griffin warmly and pleasantly, "Thank you, Grand Griffin"! The Grand Griffin then says to Stin, "Stin, you are the Monarch of the West. With this Gift, you must Guard your Kingdom against Vice in times of trouble. You will go now with Peace in your Heart and Rule with Justice, Honour and Grace."

Stin takes the Escutcheon and watches from the side. Sastia steps forward and places her hand on the Grand Griffins Talon. Her Hand turns to water a magical half-transparent half translucent Liquid glow appears. She quickly removes it and finds a multi-coloured Jewel.

The Grand Griffin, like the same as the others, tells Sastia, "Sastia Monarch of the South, you will Rule with richness and nobility, you must Guide your People in ways of Honour, Kindness and Virtue, you will Rule in Kindness, Grace, Dignity,

Honour and Justice as your People will know True Wealth in your Kingdom."

The four Monarchs stand side by side together. The Grand Griffin stands before them and extends his Wing, and says,

"Climb on my Wing and sit on my back. I will take you to your Destinations". The Grand Griffin takes them to their Destinations, where, Dwarves, Fairies, Banshees and Elves await them with Keys to their respective Castles.

The first to arrive at her Castle Kingdom is Stin. She leaves the other Monarchs and is waited by Elves who shows her around her splendid Castle. The Castle is large and surrounded by a wondrous Kingdom the size of a City. She then sits at her Throne and pleasantly Christens the Palace with her Wise Words,

"I am Stin Monarch of the West, and from this Day, this Kingdom will know of Splendour and Wealth and with my Leadership, the People. We will Live in ways of Nobility and Assurance".

Second is Tresel, who is waiting to be Fairies. She enters her Castle and goes straight to her room, where she asks the Fairies to gently sing her a Lullaby to drift her off to sleep. The Fairy flies in and says, "Okay, I am a Fairy, you know".

Fairy sings – "all is well. All is sweet; soon they'll be a wondrous treat. When the morning comes, Birds will sing and will all fly to wondrous sleep, dream away all through the day, remember the ways of Ninarphay".

"dream of the ways all through the day. Remember the ways of Ninarphay sleep away every day we pray the ways of Ninarphay will remain the same."

"value the truth, and all that is due will be given to you; respond to the inner self and your truth will be made wealth as long as you respect others and be reliable."

"give as much as you take and realise you get back what you put in, support those who support you, be free to do the right thing and with liberty and love defend the ways of Ninarphay."

"birds sing their song a sweet melody; fairies wave their fairy dust to make sweet dreams of harmony; banshees sing and feed the souls of virtue. This is Ninarphay, a place where dreams come true."

"believe in justice, respect the virtue of the law, and have justice in your heart; the community must be of value and joy, inclusive, pray to the ways of binary."

"Opportunity awaits, and we await our time patience is a virtue we must understand and aspire to the brightest day with virtue and goodness in our hearts; that is the way of Ninarphay."

"dream of the ways all through the day, remember the ways of Ninarphay, never let Ninarphays ways slip away, every day we pray the ways of Ninarphay will stay the same."

"birds sing their song a sweet melody; fairies wave their wands to make sweet dreams of harmony; banshees sing and feed the souls of virtue; this is Ninarphay, a place where dreams come true."

Tresel drifts softly to sleep and dreams as the Fairy sprinkles over her Fairy Dust.

Third is Sastia, who is waited by Dwarves. She goes straight to the Forgery Chamber and asks them to make her a crystallised Dagger to Protect them from Evil Forces if they ever invade.

"This is the Dwarf kingdom of the four Griffin Lands, and you must be the Noble Steward they've appointed".

Sastia replies, "I sure am" Standing over the Forger with a Serious expression, Sastia says, "You must make me a Dagger fit for Monarchy. It must be Rich in Splendour and have the magical qualities to ward away Evil Spirits."

The Dwarf says, sitting at his Forgers' Chair, "Right away, my Fair Lady". He begins banging his Steal forging the Dagger.

Fourth, Nivea, who is waited by Banshees, enters her Castle with her Banshee Commander and goes straight to the Kitchen, where they prepare a big Meal to get to know each other and then eat a big Feast in the Dining Hall. Nivea says, "So I Rule the Kingdom of the Banshees. I couldn't be happier with myself. I hear Banshees Sing and have great Power". Banshee's Servant replies in a subtle yet strong tone, almost as if singing, "I hope they have chosen well. You seem very Confidant as a Monarch; Banshees in this Castle adore Confidence", Nivea tells them, "Good! Because Confidence isn't the only Moral to Live by. I Pride myself on the Notion of Justice that includes Justice in everything I do, so Vice will not be tolerated. You've all been warned don't cross the line and rules. I am preparing to set out."

In an Enthusiastic tone, the Banshee's Servant says, "Yes, my Lady Justice is also a Strong Moral I have."

CHAPTER TWO

The Grand Griffins Goodwill

Inside the Grand Griffins Sky Castle, the interiors are vast and spacious. The main Doors of the actual Sky Castle are suspended in mid-air and are over 30 feet high, supported by an unimaginably tall Tower that leads to the Sky.

The Ground Entrance that leads to the Sky Castle is like any other Castle. It has splendid White and Gold interiors, Wall Paintings and many delicate and mystical ornaments.

The Ground Entrance leads up to the Sky Castle. A flight of magical Stairs leads up to a tall Tower where the Sky Castle rests.

It is the day time 10 years on from when the four Monarchs were first appointed as Regents of the four Griffin Lands of Ninarphay.

The Grand Griffin is in his Sky Castle with his Loyal Friend and Faithful Servant, the Great Sprite.

Sprites are Spirit beings with the Ordinance of Deities and great Powers of Virtue. This Sprite, in particular, stood for the Value of Fortitude.

The Grand Griffin is sitting between his four Great Pillars; in front of him is a golden Water Fountain that allows him to see all that goes on in his Kingdom Lands as he is the Soul Ruler of the Griffin Lands of Ninarphay.

In it, he finds a new Law has been passed between the four Griffin Kingdoms of Ninarphay.

All four Monarchs, Nivea of the East, Tresel of the North, Sastia of the South and Stin of the West, have agreed to this new Law, which the Grand Griffin had ruled out the "Law of Execution" the Sprite enters through the great Doors and beholds her Master as she approaches him.

The Grand Griffin looks upon the Great Sprite and says to her in a bold and discerning voice, "It appears the four Monarchs of the Griffin Lands have become Vengeful and Cruel; they have left Values of Virtue for ways of Malice I need you to help me teach them a lesson, they have passed a new Law that I deemed unacceptable, I visited them in their dreams, and still they choose to Banish my Counsel."

The Great Sprite appears Agile and Regal with a Sword at her Side and long pointy Ears similar to an Elf, but Sprites have different tendencies. Although they are not distinct like Elves to Humans or Banshees to Fairies, they have other qualities like the ability to Fly and Amazing Speed.

"Grand Griffin, my Lord and Master, what do you wish me to teach them"? The Great Sprite says to the Grand Griffin. The Grand Griffin replies, "Great Sprite, you are my most Honoured Guest and Loyal subject. You are the Fortitude of Ninarphay in my Eyes.

I entrust you with this mission to ensure the four Monarchs Learn of Gratitude and Care in all they do. They are Monarchs, and without the Gift of Morale, Monarchy is a wasted Title."

The Great Sprite says to the Griffin with a look of Seriousness and a tone of Good Conscience.

"Your Power and Wisdom are Legends throughout the Land, Grand Griffin. You are known for many Feats and Marvels over the Centuries through your long and eventful Life".

"I am but your humble and gracious Servant. You have bequeathed me with great Powers and Responsibilities, so I ask, what do you want me to do, Grand Griffin?"

The Grand Griffin tells her of her Quest, he says to the Great Sprite. "You will retrieve my Gifts from them and lure them here to my Castle, where they will each face Trail for their Sins against my Noble Orders."

The Great Sprite with an Attitude of Confidence says to the Grand Griffin. "I am awaiting your Instructions". The Grand Griffin then proceeds to tell her.

"Go to the Eastern Wood. You will find the Monarch of the East at her Eastern retreat, retrieve my Sword of the East, and bring it back here. After you visit the Tea House in the North, you will find Sandals bearing my Insignia belonging to the Monarch of the North.

Then go to South of the Kingdom, where the Monarch of the South has my Insignia Jewel in her main Bank Vault. Use all of your Cunning and Wit to outsmart her.

Finally, you must visit the Monarch of the West and retrieve my Escutcheon where she has left it on Display at her Favourite Shop."

The Great Sprite says to the Grand Griffin. "The Monarch of the West should know better a Favoured Shop in the Middle of the Kingdom, how careless of her".

The Grand Griffin replies, "She lacks Discipline and Personal Restraint. How careless, indeed. Now be on your way Great Sprite and take some Money and Water with you. Make haste!"

The Great Sprite exits the Door and begins her long and Arduous Journey through the Long and Wide Valleys, Forest Woods and Briars of the Griffin Lands of Ninarphay.

CHAPTER THREE

The Great Sprites Journey

In the Northern Valley of the Woods, she encounters a Witch in a Curry House who has a Lycanthrope constantly stealing her Cattle; she stays there Overnight and, instead of Gold, offers her Protection as Payment.

She spends the Night slaying the Lycanthrope and cooking her Curry, leaving her with Gold. She thanks her and Gifts her a Gift of Potion in return.

It's early morning, and the Sprite arrives in the Eastern Wood, where she overhears Ogres, who have escaped from Transzalore, plotting on Nivea. The Ogres sit in a Cave and discuss what they will do.

The most significant turns to the others and says, "I heard that Nivea Dolly's a Monarch now." The second one says. "They sure have come a long way since they were Guests in our Temple; in that lovely Dungeon, we kept them and gave them a Block of Wood to feast on. Weren't those the Good Old Days?

I bet they're rotting in their Boots, wishing to get back." The third and ugliest says, "That Nivea hurt my Mummy. I didn't see her again after that." The biggest one yet again says.

"I've spotted where she's hiding just a Mile away from here. In a minute, we'll sneak in, knock her over the Head with a Block of Wood and take her back through the Portal to Transzalore, where she can pick my Feet."

It's Daytime, and the Ogres arrive at the Forest Hut, where Nivea is practising with her Sword. They call her out, and in a rage, Nivea slays them.

The Monarch of the East Nivea is fighting in the Forest; she slays three Ogres, then gets her Servant to lay the Sword in a Scabbard and Place it high on the wall to the entrance of the Spa House.

Nivea tells her Servant from her Tea Room in a fit of Tears. "You have no idea what it was like being held Captive in the Temple of Remorse.

"A family of Donned Ogres Spoilt, Horrible, Yucky and Disgusting." The banshee Servant retorts, "Were those their names?" Nivea replies, "And their mannerisms."

The Great Sprite is watching outside from a Distance, scoping out the surroundings and observing the Intentions and Methods of the Eastern Monarch, ensuring what she is doing is in the Correct Attitude.

The Monarch goes Upstairs, leaving her Sword with the Servant; the Great Sprite decides it is time for her to take the Sword.

The Monarch sits down in an Upstairs Room to eat a Meal. Nivea says, "Those Ogres sure make you work up a Morning Appetite O'well, here we go, then second Breakfast."

Nivea is fighting back the Sorrow with Words of Encouragement and a Notion of Goodwill.

The Sprite sneaks from behind the wall, walks into the House, unsuspectingly jumps up high, swipes the Sword, and makes a quick Exit. The Banshee Servant calls out to Nivea, "Nivea!" Nivea quickly grabs her Dagger and chases after the Sprite, who is too fast for her.

Nivea shouts, "Oi, you get back here with my Sword, you Wicked, Wicked little Sprite. I'll have you put down for this!" The Great Sprite calls, "Too late. I'm running, and you can't catch a running Sprite, especially this one."

The Great Sprite disappears into the distance. Nivea shouts to her Servant, "Send a Pigeon to find that Sprite".

The Great Sprite makes her Great getaway to an Inn where she encounters a Wizard who is swindling people out of their Fortunes through magical Craft. The Wizard owns the Inn, and whenever someone Books to stay, they Forfeit their Wealth to him.

A Banshee Warrior tells her of all the Poor Villagers nearby that have Suffered his Wrath, taking her away from the Inn and into his Home to Sleep.

The next day the Great Sprite decides she will do something about it, so she gathers the Sword and battles the Wizard. The Sword has Great Charm, but the Wizard is Powerful.

The Great Sprite remembers the Potion the Witch gave to her. She takes it out of her Satchel and pours it on the Wizard. The Wizard dissolves, and all the Towns People re-inherit their Wealth.

The Great Sprite spends the rest of the day resting in the Inn. In the morning, she returns on her Quest, travelling to the Tea House in the North Kingdom of the Griffin Lands of Ninarphay.

The Great Sprite arrives at the Tea House and watches the movements of the Northern Monarch from a Distance.

The Monarch of the North rests inside her Tea House, which has a Comfortable Carpet.

The Sprite, yet again, looks on from behind a Wall. The Monarch slips out of her Sandals and walks towards the Kitchen area, where Comfier Carpet is yet again.

She goes to the Oven and takes out Wonderful Sandal Shaped Biscuits from the Biscuit Oven she had prepared. She arranges them evenly on the Cooling Tray and prepares a Special Drink.

The Sprite noticing she's Distracted and away from her Sandals, seizes her Chance. She runs towards the Tea House and opens the Door, and as quickly as she opens the Door, she takes the Sandals and runs as the Door closes behind her.

The Monarch Chases after her, but she gets away. She gets her Lazy Maid, who is Reluctant, Spoilt and Stubborn, to send a Tracker Cat, which she eventually does.

On the way to see the Monarch of the South, the Great Sprite stays in a Dwarf Forger's Inn, where she encounters a scene.

A Dwarf has had his Weapons that he recently Forged taken by a Dark Lord who put him under a Trance. After arguing, he agrees to make more Weapons for him.

The Great Sprite talks to the Dwarf about his Situation, the Dwarf tells her he had reported to the Monarch of his Situation, but she was more concerned about Procuring Wealth.

The Great Sprite tells him, "Send a Message to the Dark Lord telling him to meet me for a Dual Tomorrow at Noon; the Dwarf sends one of his Helpers to tell the Dark Lord; the Dark Lord accepts the Challenge."

The next day the Great Sprite and the Dark Lord meet for a Dual. The Great Sprite introduces herself, telling the Dark Lord she is the Protector of these Lands.

The Dark Lord Retorts by telling her his plans for the Land. He tells the Great Sprite, "I am Dark Lord Zenith Ogre, King of Transzalore.

I have returned for the four Crowns that were taken from me, I am preparing my Ogre Army, and once I have retrieved the four Sacred Keys from the Land of Griffin, I will open a Portal large enough to invade."

The Great Sprite realises. "Oh no, that's what the Lycan and the Wizard were after; the Witch has a Sacred Key, and so do the Riches of the Banshee's Village."

The two Creatures begin to Dual. The Great Sprite wins, and the Dark Lord is Wounded and disappears into a Cloud of Black Soot.

The Monarch of the South is sitting on her Throne, talking to her Generals about Enriching the Kingdom.

Sastia tells them, "We must find a new export to Enrich the Kingdom. It can be Food, Cloth Material and even a Jewel. Can anyone in this Court do such a thing?" In the Court, there are many Town Folk. The Sprite steps forward and presents a magical Tassel with the Power to weave Cloth into an Item of Clothing in a minute.

Sastia looks upon the Great Sprite with a Pleasing Awe and says, "And who might you be?" Great Sprite replies, "I am the Great Sprite Servant of the Grand Griffin who lives in the Sky Castle at the Centre of the four Griffin Kingdoms of Ninarphay. I Come Bearing Gifts."

Sastia takes the Tassel and looks upon it. She shakes it, and two Pairs of Beautiful looking Socks instantly weave.

Sastia then, with more amazement than before, says to the Great Sprite. "It has the Grand Griffins Hallmarks. We must be very Lucky if you came here on this Glorious Day, and what must we do to Enter into this Trade Deal?"

The Great Sprite replies, "First, you must let me see the Jewel the Grand Griffin bestowed on you on the day of your inauguration. Then we can Trade until your Heart's Content."

With minimum haste, the Southern Monarch reaches into her Pocket, unlocks a Box, and extends the Key to the Sprite without delay or Problem.

Sastia tells the Great Sprite the Key is in the Central Vault of the Main Bank. Two of my Guards will accompany you there. The Sprite takes the Key.

The two Guards and the Sprite arrive at the Central Bank Vault. They walk towards the entrance; the Vault is guarded by a Magic Door and two great Axes on either Side.

The Great Sprite is in the Bank Vault with the Key. She gets shown to the Main Safe along with the Guards.

She opens the Vault and beholds the Jewel. She quickly fights the Guards off and runs away with the Jewel. The two Guards chase her.

On the way to see the Monarch of the West, the Great Sprite comes across a Group of Fairies in the Woods.

They tell her an Evil Goblin is trying to steal their Magic, and every night, he raids the Sanctity of their Wood, looking for the source of their Powers.

The Great Sprite tells them by her Tent and Camp Fire Tonight, when he comes, she'll lay a Trap and slay him.

The Night draws in, and the Evil Goblin appears as the Great Sprite waits in the Tree. By the Briar, there is a Flower Garden with Plants that look like Jewels.

The Goblin approaches it. As he gets close, the Sprite tugs on a Rope, and the Goblin falls to the Ground.

The Sprite tells him, "Your days of Evil are done; you should have never tried to take what does not belong to you." The Great Sprite slays the Evil Goblin.

The Western Monarch is lying in her Bed laughing at a Fat Lady in a Bed full of filthy food.

In the Central Castle Shop, the Escutcheon is Suspended in Mid-Air, guarded by Magical Seals that are unbreakable unless she lifts the Spell Personally or is broken by Default.

The Sprite wonders in looking for it. She walks towards the Shop Clerk, and the Great Sprite asks, "How much for that Escutcheon?"

The Shop Clerk replies, "It could cost you your Soul." Great Sprite says, "How much in Money?"

Shop Clerk responds, "A Priceless Jewel and your Address, and even then, you couldn't afford it."

With a look of certainty, the Great Sprite exclaims to the Clerk, "Why!" The Shop Clerk points down at her rolling her Fingers and pointing towards herself, leans in and tells the Great Sprite. "It is guarded by two Magical Seals. One is the Price of your Address. The other is the price of a priceless Jewel."

The Great Sprite also leans in and, with a Devious smile, says, "What if I was to break that Spell?"

The Shop Clerk breaks the Cycle of Mysterious looks and goes Back to the usual way of speaking, saying, "Then you'll own the Escutcheon."

The Sprite gives the Shop Clerk the Grand Griffins Address and presents the Jewel.

The Spell breaks, and the Sprite grabs her Reward gathering the Jewel along with it. She makes a quick Exit.

A Fairy awakens the Western Monarch and says, "Madam, a Sprite has broken in and taken your Escutcheon to the Griffin's Castle." Stin, the Western Monarch, replies, "What, I must go there at once. Fetch me my Musket."

CHAPTER FOUR

The Four Monarchs' Rebellion

The next day arrives inside the Grand Griffins Castle, and the Grand Griffin receives the Gifts he gave to the Monarchs from the Great Sprite.

He looks into his Water Fountain and realises the four Monarchs are riding Side by Side, approaching his Sky Castles Ground Entrance just as he intended.

Nivea of the East is carrying a Lock, Chain and Sword. Tresel Monarch of the North is taking a Poisoned Bow and Arrow. Sastia Monarch of the South is carrying a Whip and Charmed Dagger. Stin Monarch of the West is carrying her Musket.

The Grand Griffin turns to the Great Sprite and says. "You must confront them and lore them here to the four Great Pillars."

It is Mid-Morning, and the four Monarchs demand to be let into the Castles Ground Entrance standing Outside. The Grand Griffins Castle Doors open, and the four Monarchs dismount and enter.

They walk through the Castle Hall Confidently and without much bother in search of their Gifts.

Nivea is the first to catch sight of the Sprite. She chases her through a Door into a Passageway that leads to a Maze.

The Sprite echoes through the swirling Maze that only she and the trusted folk of the Castle are accustomed to. "If you can find your way to the Centre of the Maze, I'll return your Sword."

Nivea makes it to the End of the Maze, where the Sprite is inevitably waiting. They have a Sword Fight, and the Sprite wins, taking her Damaged Body Back to the Griffins Pillars to lay on the Plinth of the four Grand Pillars by the Grand Griffin.

The three remaining Monarchs continue walking through the Grand Castle, which is as big as a small City but as homely and crowded as an average-sized House.

Tresel spots the Great Sprite run up a flight of Stairs; she follows her into an Art Room, where she is greeted by a Goblin painting a Portrait.

Tresel She says to the Goblin, "Who are you?" The Goblin responds, "I'm the Castle Curator!" Tresel sits at the Table beside him and begins a conversation, "What are you doing." Tresel asks.

The Goblin replies painting a Picture! "Sit down, eat some Fruit. The Griffin is awaiting you." Tresel turns her nose away from the Fruit, saying, "Okay, but I won't trust the Food."

With a Grim look, the Goblin says, "You're going to have this until Paint makes you thirsty, and the first time you Smell it, forgetful." The Goblin and Tresel talk about Trust and the Grand Griffin. From behind, the Great Sprite pours a Drink which Tresel unsuspectingly drinks. She falls Unconscious and becomes consumed by the Painting. She joins Nivea in the Throne Room in her respective Corner.

Stin Monarch of the West sees the Sprite go through a secret Passageway, and she follows her. They arrive at a Library.

An Elf awaits her. The Library Elf says, "Put away you're Whip and Daggers. You're in my library. You will Obey my Rules." The Elf says in a stern and condescending Tone.

Stin tells the Elf with an Arrogant yet Strong Tone, "This is a Time of War Rules will be broken." The Elf, in a calm yet unsettled way, says to Stin. "Suit yourself. Since you're in a Library, I suggest you read a Book."

Stin says, "Okay!" Stin opens a Book, and she passes out just from the Page's Dust. The Great Sprite takes her to the Grand Griffin. She lies in her respective Corner of the Throne Room.

One left and Stin wonders through the Castle until she came to the Grand Griffin's Throne Room; at three of the four Pillars lay each of the three Monarchs to their respective Corners.

Stin tells the Grand Griffin in a convincing Tone, "The only Pillar left is to the West of the Grand Griffins Throne Perch." The Grand Griffin replies, "Surely, now you face your Judgement." The fourth Monarch drops her Musket and says. "It's Over!"

The Grand Griffin uses the Power of his Claw to tie the remaining Monarch to the Western Pillar of his Throne Room Perch. Now the four Monarchs lay on the floor in their respective Corner Pillar with their once Treasured Gifts in front of them.

The Great Sprite tells the four Monarchs collectively. Your ungratefulness was Wicked, and now you must resolve the Wishes of the Grand Griffin. The four Monarchs apologise, saying. "We are Eternally sorry, Grand Griffin; please forgive us!"

The Grand Griffin speaks, "You have been Gifted with Worldly Responsibility and True Luxury, but you Abused this Gift. You were told to have a Life of Justice and a Heart of Mercy; instead, you choose Revenge and Dishonour. For this, you must pay a Costly Price.

"Power and Wealth must Attribute Honour and Decency. You may never have the Will to Govern again if you have not learnt this.

You shall all be sealed in your respective Pillars for your Crimes, realising the Morals of your Virtue for Eternity."

The Grand Griffin stamps his Mighty Paw, and the Monarchs and their Chains and Gifts vanish into the Pillars, leaving behind a decorative golden Wall Tassel on each Magical Marble Pillar.

After the Sprite and Grand Griffin imprison the four Monarchs, she tells the Grand Griffin of her escapades, slaying the Lycan, immobilising the Wizard, Slaying the Ogres and her encounter with Dark Lord Zenith of Transzalore.

The Great Sprite tells the Grand Griffin, "I encountered five Transzaloreons."

The Grand Griffin responds. "The four Monarchs must be Responsible. Their Ill-natured ways must have tipped the

Balance and torn a Rift in-between the Realms. This is what happens when Powerful Ninarphaians are not kind to Ninarphay." "Do tell me more"! Says the Grand Griffin.

The Great Sprite speaks. "The Ogres spoke of a Special Key, and Dark Lord Zenith escaped and is believed to be raising an Army to invade the Griffin Lands of Ninarphay in search of the four Monarchs; he called them the four Crowns." "Yes, they are Special, but we'll save the Reasons for being chosen till later", Says the Grand Griffin.

"I met a Witch, a Dwarf, a Banshee, and a Fairy." Grand Griffin asks. "Will they help stop Dark Lord Zenith's Evil Forces?"

Great Sprite in a voice of hope says. "I hope so. I overheard him speak of the Portal not being big enough to support his Army and that he was getting more Portal Keys."

The Grand Griffin tells the Sprite. "We'll save the Suspense for another Time. We gather these Noble Ninarphaians in the morning, but Tonight gets some Rest."

THE END

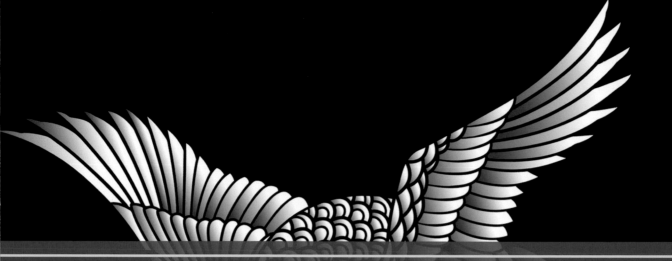

NINARPHAY TALES VOL. II

The Rat, The Rabbit, The Blue River Phoenix And The Shark Lady

The Nine Rings

A Rat and Rabbit Sprite are running through Aquarium Tower at the Centre of Transzalore along with a Blue River Phoenix.

Each carries three Giant Gold Rings, and the Phoenix has a golden Sceptre.

Sepvrein the Shark Lady and her two Accomplice, Sinchinty, the Alligator Lord, and Nevreum, the Octopus Lord of the Dark Seas of Transzalore.

They run through water lined Brown Floor with a Black Walled Hallway.

They reach the End of the Hallway and come to a Window while running the Blue River Phoenix in a show of Power blasts through the Window, and the three Ninarphaians take flight.

They fly Over the Black Seas with the Rabbit and Rat holding on to the long Legs of the Blue River Phoenix.

The Phoenix says, "Hang on tight"! Rain is falling, and the Sea is rough.

The Shark, with her Guile's breathing air, jumps through the Air towards the Phoenix and her Comrades as the Phoenix reaches for her Sceptre, the Blue River Phoenix says.

"Sceptre of Light Water and Air take our Kin and us back to Ninarphays Leer."

A Golden Triangle appears, and the three Ninarphaians and the Seas are transported.

They arrive in Ninarphay, and the nine Rings are aligned and Suspended in Mid – Air.

A Water Valley is created between two Forests, and a magical Bridge is slowly built, but before they can cross into Ninarphay, the Shark Lady appears, and the Magic Bridge stops assembling. The two Sprites turn to the Phoenix and say.

"Lady Phoenix, what's happening?" Blue Phoenix tells the Rat and the Rabbit.

"The Magic of Ninarphay will not work whilst a Dark Lord of Transzalore obstructs it".

The Rabbit asks, "So what do we do now?" The Blue River Phoenix says, "Wait here for me to defeat this Shark Lady; an Elf shall appear, and for every Game Won Lost or Forfeited, he will through a Magic Trinket, Ornament or Jewel into the Lake for Transzalore or on the Land for Ninarphay.

I will be Suspended in Mid-Air, but I will be an Astral Projection across the nine Kingdom Realms of Ninarphay, restoring the Rings and Fresh, Clean Water to the Kingdoms.

Wait to cross until I have returned. Heed my Wise and Glorious Words, and you'll have Harmony and Riches beyond your belief." An Elf appears across the Bridge carrying a Pot of Gold, Jewels, Ornaments and Trinkets.

The Rat Sprite tells The Blue River Phoenix, "Blue River Phoenix, who is that Elf?" The Blue River Phoenix tells him. "That is the Architect of the Bridge.

He is here to amend your Riches after you cross. Now wait here and remember my Words."

The Blue River Phoenix flies over the Shark Infested Water where the Rings are lying still and dormant on the River.

The Shark Lady is immersed in the water and trapped in a Circle.

The Shark Lady tells the River Phoenix. "Lady Phoenix Ruler of the four Phoenix Lands of Ninarphay, I Challenge you to a Clash of Wills; whoever wins keeps the so-needed Water."

The Blue River Phoenix replies. "Lady Shark, give up. You are not in Transzalore anymore."

Shark lady replies. "I know, but if I could get that Sceptre, I could reverse all the Water Spells instantly, take the Rings closer to me and leave for Transzalore."

Without haste, the Blue River Phoenix acts. "Fine, I Challenge you to nine Clashes of Will in the nine Kingdom Lands of Ninarphay!"

The Blue River Phoenix Castes the Sceptre and waves it over the River inciting a Mantra.

"Transmission freeze Sceptres time in Ninarphay's Fountains Design!" A flash appears over the Sea, and the two Creatures remain Suspended in Mid-Air.

CHAPTER TWO

Battle In The Banshees Tavern

The Rat and Rabbit Sprite watch!

They are transported to the Griffin Lands Banshee Temple, where they Enter a Cooks Tavern.

The Tavern is Large and Spacious enough to House around one thousand Banshees. There are golden Ornaments and Wondrous Décor with Comfortable Chairs and Tables with Food in front of them.

They stand at the entrance of the Tavern, and to their rear is a large Fountain with a Statue of two twin Banshees on the exterior Décor, one from Ninarphay and one from Transzalore.

The owner of the Tavern is a Banshee Cook. She turns to them and says. "Can I help you?" The Phoenix says.

"Were hear about the Fountain!" The Shark Lady retorts, "I'm here to claim it."

The Cook replies. "Oh yes, about that 30-foot Fountain that just appeared a few minutes ago. I was pleased to know that it was to help with the Water Supply."

"We in the Banshee temple worship Virtue and Justice as our way of Life and are taught to help all who come into our Care.

Phoenix Lord of the four Phoenix Lands, we have been praying for this day. What can I do to help you?" The Blue River Phoenix tells her.

"Go to the Fountains Basin and retrieve a Scroll. It will tell us what we have to do for this Challenge."

"Yes, most Beautiful Blue River Phoenix." says the Cook.

She flies over to the Fountain and retrieves the Scroll. On the Scroll, there are Instructions she reads.

"The answer is in the Fountain!" The two Twin Banshees become animated and begin to move. They soon start speaking. "I am the Banshee Fountain of Ninarphay!"

"And I am the Banshee Fountain of Transzalore! You each have the task of winning the Gold Ring for the Fountain. For this, you must Cultivate, Work and fight as is the Law of Purification.

Now your Challenge to the Fountain, eat ten Plates, wash them, and fight for the Ring. Your Challenge begins now!" "Good Luck, Ninarphay!"

"Good Luck Transzalore!" The two Twin Figures restate to their Natural State. The Fountain sprouts Clear Water, and the Challenge begins. The Banshee cook turns to the Phoenix and Shark saying.

"I will Cook you each ten Meals when you're done. Wash them in the Fountain, then battle for the force of nine Fountain Rings."

The two Lords take a Seat and await their first Meal. The Blue River Phoenix Tells the Shark Lady.

"Sepvrein, I am destined to Win each of these battles. In Transzalore, I am more Powerful, and in Ninarphay, doubly, so I will not think less of you if you make sense and Forfeit." The Shark Lady replies.

"Surrender is for Cowards. I believe in Destiny, but I also believe in Chance."

The first plate is presented, and they begin to eat the Phoenix Wins the first plate along with the second, third, fourth, fifth, sixth, seventh, eighth, ninth and tenth.

The Blue River Phoenix finishes her plate whilst the Shark Lady lags behind on her ninth. The Phoenix flies to the Golden 30-foot Fountain and begins her second task.

At first, the Fountain runs free; then, the Transzalore Side stops the water. The Phoenix complains saying.

"The Water cannot just stop. That's cheating." The Ninarphay side shrugs at the Transzalore side, and water begins running again. The Shark finishes her plate and leaps 30 feet holding her Dishes. She then begins her task.

The Phoenix finishes her Dishes, and a Gold Ring materialises. The Ninarphay Tap congratulates her, saying.

"Congratulations, Blue River Phoenix Leader of the four Phoenix Lands, you have Won the first task.

Now place the Golden Ring in the Fountain Centre, and we will remain in Ninarphay." The Transzalore Fountain says, "It's just rotten Luck, that's all."

CHAPTER THREE

Sprite Spa Houses

The Sceptre reappears, there is a Bright Flash, and the two Rivals move on to their next task.

The Sceptre reappears in the Sky of the Sprite Lands, and a Grey Stone Fountain is decorated with several Sprites and Plant Reefs.

The Phoenix and the Shark appear in the Sprites Spa HoShe says they look outside a Window, and a Female Sprite begins to talk to says. "I received a Scroll a Day ago telling me you would appear and I should present a Challenge.

So here we go; you must collect these three things and bring them to the Fountain, where you will leave them on the Reef Pillars. The first to complete this task will receive a Gold Ring.

You must find a Magic Scented Oil on the Ground Floor, Acupuncture Needles on the 1st floor, and a Golden Flower on the third floor.

Your task begins now." They spot the Scented Oils and fight each other for the Box. When the Shark Lady opens the Box, she is confronted by Marbles.

They see a Shoebox, the Phoenix opens it, and inside are Magical Scented Oils. She ascends to the Next Level, and the Shark Lady follows behind, climbing the Stairs.

By Time the Shark gets to the Next Level, the Phoenix finds a Wall Case displaying Acupuncture Needles. As she goes for it, the Shark grabs her from behind, stealing the Needles. She advances to the final Level.

They get to the final Level simultaneously, and both have to search through Rooms to find the Reef. They search for a Library, a Utility Room, a Bathroom and a Spa Room Lounge.

Finally, they get to a Lounge where they spot a Case holding a Reef.

They Battle each other intensely for all three of the items. In the end, the Phoenix is booming, and she progresses to the Fountain, where she lays the items on the Stone Reef of the Fountain.

The Waters begin to Spring, the Sprite cheers, and the Sceptre reappears.

CHAPTER FOUR

Grandios Museum

The Sceptre reappears in the Goblin Lands, and the Bright Light appears and flashes again.

The Phoenix and Shark reappear in a Grand Museum. They wander through the Museum in search of the Fountain.

Directly Outside the Museum in the Garden area is a 30-foot Black Metallic Fountain decorated with many Scholars' like Goblins tasselled on the Steel Structure.

At the Back Entrance of the Museum inside stands a Goblin. The Goblin stands in Front of the Phoenix and Shark by the entrance and says.

"What are you Ladies doing here?" The Phoenix replies. "I am the Blue River Phoenix Grand Lord of the Phoenix Lands." The Shark replies. "I am a Sepvrein Shark Lord of Transzalore."

The Goblin then proceeds to say. "Stop there. I know where you're going with this; wait there." The Goblin pulls out a Scroll from his Pocket and says.

"Before you go any further, these are the Goblin Lands of Ninarphay, Famed for our Begrudging Preservation of Historical events, Treasuring of Relics and thousands of Museums."

The Blue River Phoenix states! "I know about the Categorical priceless keep of Goblin Lands, but please, good Goblin, tell us of our Challenge." The Goblin replies.

"Okay, only to let you know this is the Grandiose Minos Museum of Ninarphay, and I am its Curator. Your Challenge is to find a Key to the Back Door and turn it in the Lock Shaft of the Steel Fountain.

Whoever Wins this Challenge Wins the Gold Ring. Good luck, and remember, it could be anywhere in this Mile-long Museum." The Goblin picks out a Key from his Back Pocket, opens a magical Door, and disappears.

The two Creatures split up and run in opposite directions in search of the Key. The Shark Lady comes to a Sign Post saying she is in the Ancient Keys area.

The Phoenix comes to the same Sign Post at the opposite end, saying she is in the Ancient Keys area. They both Enter the same Area from Opposite Sides.

They Enter the Dark Lit Room. The Abyss Key Room is a darkly lit room filled with thousands of Keys and details of their Origins.

She finds a Scroll saying the Key to the Fountain is in this room. The Phoenix comes to the same room and reads the same Scroll saying the same thing from the other end.

The Key is at the Centre of the large and continuous Room. The room is so big that they don't see each other.

They walk towards the Centre of the Room. As they go from one end to the Other, they continuously search the Rooms Inventory of Keys.

They finally get to the Centre of the Room, and the final Key says Ninarphays, Transzalores Fountain Key.

They Battle each other over the Key. Finally, the Phoenix Wins the Battle; the room spins, and suddenly, they are standing in the Garden facing the Fountain. The Phoenix enters the Key into the Fountain.

A Gold Ring is revealed to her. She inserts it into the Centre of the Fountain, and water begins to run. The Goblin says! "Well done, Blue River Phoenix. Now Fresh Clean Water will run through the Goblin Lands of Ninarphay".

The Sceptre reappears in the Sky. A Bright Flash flashes and transports them to their next Location.

CHAPTER FIVE

Education City

The Sceptre reappears, and Flashes in the Sky and the Pair are transported to the Elf Lands Education City.

They walk in through the Entrance of the main Education Centre and approach the Principle of the Lands, an Elf called Principal Hawk.

He is holding a Scroll in his Hands and finishes reading it.

He says to them! "I am the Head Master Elf Principal Hawk. I have three Challenges for you both. Each one you Win, you will Gain a Golden Ring.

Writing a five-page Dossier on the Principles of your Land is the first of your three Challenges. Whomsoever Paper shows the most Factual and Theoretical Truth will receive the first of the three Gold Rings.

The second is a Maths Quiz. Whomsoever has the best mathematical ability and scores highest on the Quiz will again Gain the Gold Ring.

Third is a Gym Challenge pitting your Martial Arts Skills to the Test. Whomsoever wins this Challenge will get the Gold Ring and inevitably be the victor of the Education Challenge."

Principal hands both the Ladies a Monitor Sheet detailing the Locations of their Classrooms where they will take the Education Challenge.

They walk down the Corridor to the Location. The interior of the Building is filled with decorative Marble and Paintings of Past Scholars.

Looking outside of the Window, they see the 30-foot Fountain Structure. The Fountain is made of shining and gleaming Silver with decorative Tassels of two female elves holding Bows and Arrows.

They enter the Classroom where a Vice Principle is waiting for them. "I am Vice Principal Formel. I will be your Tutor. In front of you is a Pen and Paper.

You have 15 minutes to write a five-page 2000-word Dossier on the Principles of your Respective Realms, Transzalore and Ninarphay! Begin!"

15 minutes later, they finish and hand in their work. Formel checks their work and then gives them their score. She tells them!

"Blue Phoenix maximum marks you have written 2000 words exactly and detailed in great Stature all of Ninarphays Prime Principles.

Great! Shark Lady, you have done the same on Transzalore, except you have yet to write precisely 2000 words. Unfortunately, this means you have Lost the Task.

Blue River Phoenix, I am Awarding you the Gold Ring." The Ring appears, and the two rivals disappear to their next task.

They reappear in the same room, and in front of them is another Test Paper.

Formel tells them! "this is the second Test. Whoever Wins this gets the second Gold Ring. A Maths Quiz, there are ten Questions on your Sheet, Theoretical and Brain busting.

These are our most complex sums; you have ten minutes. Begin!"

The two rivals toil over the Paper. Ten minutes later, Formel tells them their Scores.

"Shark Lady, you got two right! Blue River Phoenix, you got three, right? Blue River Phoenix, you Win the Ring!"

Principal Hawk approaches the room and says. "Blue River Phoenix, you have Won both Challenges, Shark Lady; therefore, you are a Forfeit."

They walk Outside, and the Blue River Phoenix inserts the Rings into the Fountain. A third one appears in the Basin of the Fountain, and water runs in the Elf Lands.

The Sceptre reappears in the Sky, a Great Golden flash appears, and the Rivals are transported.

CHAPTER SIX

The Dwarf Kingdom

They are transported to their next Battle. The Sceptre reappears and Flashes in the Sky, and they appear in a Mansion Castle. They are surrounded by Statues, Weapons, Relics and Golden Jewelled Ornaments.

They walk down the long winding Grand Corridor until they come to a Throne Room, where they are greeted by a Dwarf on a Throne.

She tells them. "I am Dwarf Fantasy. I am the Governess of these Parts. You will be given three Challenges Cook, Forge and Battle. Whoever wins will receive three Gold Rings. Begin!"

They appear in a Food Court and are told to Cook an Evening Meal.

They Cook a Feast and share it with the Governess and her Court Guards. The Governess then decides whose food tastes the nicest.

"Sepvrein, your Food is Sour and Dull, but Grand River Phoenix, your Food is Imaginative and Tasty."

They turn to see the Nickel Fountain at the Back of the Court. "The next Challenge is to Forge an Axe. After this, you will go into Battle using that Forged Axe for your final Challenge. Begin!"

The Dwarf slams her Staff on the Ground, and they are transported to a Forgers Chamber. They each Forge an Axe and then show it to the Governor's Court.

The Governor checks the Axes and says. "It's clear whose Won this the golden Ring goes again to the River Phoenix.

Time for your third and final Challenge to the Battle Axe Arena." The Dwarf Bangs her Staff on the Ground, and they are transported to an Arena.

Fantasy says! "Let the final Challenge begin." A Buzzer sounds, and the Battle-axe Challenge begins. They Battle three Rounds with the Axe, and in the final round, Sepvrein Axe breaks, and The Grand River Phoenix is Awarded Victory.

CHAPTER SEVEN

Fairies Pavilion

The Nickel Fountain runs, the Sceptre reappears, and they are transported to the Fairies Pavilion.

In the Fairy Kingdom, they are greeted by Grand Fairy Esmeral. The Fountain in the Fairy Kingdom is 30-foot Marble with Beautiful Fairies tasselled around it. "I am Esmeral, Guardian of this Land. You have a Water Challenge to find the three golden Rings.

One is in the Flower River, one is Located in the Pond Stream, and the final one you will have to Fight for. Good luck!"

The Fairy waves her Wand, and they appear in a Giant Frogs Pond.

They spot the first Ring Floating on top of a Lotus Pond. They swim and Fly towards it, but as they are about to take it, the Frog uses his Tongue and snatches it away.

They chase the Frog as it jumps along the Lotu's Leaves. Finally, they catch the Frog and Wrestle for the Ring.

The Phoenix gets the Ring, and finally, Esmeral reappears. "well done, Grand Blue River Phoenix, you have Won the first Challenge. Time for your second Challenge."

The Fairy waves her Wand, and they are transported to a River Bed. They dive into the water and swim to the Bottom. At the Bottom of the River is a Treasure Chest.

They race to the Treasure Chest and begin searching through it. The Grand Phoenix finds the Gold Ring and Wins the Challenge yet again.

They are soon transported to a solid Marble Tree House. Esmeral says! "now it's Time for your final Battle. Whoever Wins this gets the final Ring.

In the Centre of the Room is a Gold Ring. You must Wrestle each other for it. Begin!"

They Wrestle each other for the Ring, and the Phoenix is Successful.

She places the three Rings at the Centre of the Marble Fountain Water begins flowing.

The Sceptre reappears in the Sky. A flash appears, and they are transported.

CHAPTER EIGHT

Search For The Sea Nymph

They are transported to a Boat Harbour in the Nymph Lands. They see the White Stone Marble Fountain in the Middle of the Harbour. They board a Boat and are Greeted by Captain Justice Raven, Pirate Reaper of the Ninarphay Seas.

He tells them! "I'm Captain Justice Raven, and I am the Captain of this Ship. For your next Challenge! You will be given three Tasks when this Ship sets sail. You will search the Haul, scrub the Decks and Orientate. The best task will be Awarded by the Sea Nymph who lives on the Boat and commands the Sea."

The Boat sets sail, and the first Challenge begins. "The first one to find the Sea Nymph in the Haul Wins." The Sea Nymph hides under a Wooden Panel behind a Container in the Haul. The two rivals begin their search.

They search high and low, far and wide, even stepping over the Sea Nymph, but they never find her. Finally, the Phoenix spots something where the Shark Lady is hiding. She ushers her away using her Cunning, then uncovers the Sea Nymph, who Awards her the Ring.

They move on to the next task. "scrub the Deck from Port to Starboard. Whoever crosses over Port and Starboard first Wins." They scrub for hours, constantly checking over their Backs with all Tasks. Naturally, the Phoenix Lady finishes first and is Awarded the Ring.

The final Challenge is Orienteering in the Captain's Cabin. They are each given a Map, Compass and Clues to find the Gold Ring in the Captain's Cabin.

They search, scan and scour the Map. Finally, the Phoenix is Successful, and she finds the Ring under a Secret Compartment of the Captain's Desk.

The Phoenix uses her Skill to Pilot the Ship Back to Shore and Place the three Rings into the Fountain. Water runs and Cleanses the Sea. The Sea Nymph sees the Phoenix.

"Thank you, Grand Blue River Phoenix. Now we have Purifying Water; the Seas will be Cleansed of Impurities Forever."

The Sceptre reappears and transports them to their following Location. The Sceptre Flashes and the two Rivals appear in the Witches Realm.

CHAPTER NINE

High Witch Limeade

They meet Great Witch Limeade, known for her Musical Talents. She is playing the Piano with a Scroll hovering above her. Outside of her Window is a 30-foot Platinum Tower. Limeade turns to them and says. "I am High Lady Witch Limeade. I Rule this Pavilion, and I have been Charged with giving you the task of winning a Gold Ring to Activate or take away the Fountain. Your mission is to find three items and Cast a Stichomancy Spell to make the Ring Materialize.

You will need to gather a Wand, Bark and a Scroll to Cast a Spell." The Shark Lady asks! "where do we find these things?" Great Witch Limeade replies. "Go into the Market and Figure it out. You have one Hour!"

The Witch waves her Wand, and the two rivals magically appear in the densely packed Witches Market. The Stools are Magic, the Products Enchanted and the Occupants Charmed.

They first try out the Magic Stools. "Excuse me, can I purchase a Scroll here?" Says the Phoenix. "No, you didn't ask properly. Try somewhere else!" Says the Stool Merchant. The Shark Lady laughs and tries the same thing but gets the same response.

They walk through the same Market for 20 minutes receiving the same Advice.

They separate with the Phoenix realising something. She reappears at the first Stool but pulls a Coin from her Ear this time.

The Witch then agrees to the purchase. She gets the second and third Items realising the Shark Lady is Right behind her. They soon reappear in the Witches High Lady Limeade Luxurious Villa.

High Lady Limeade says to them. "You were 45 minutes Grand Lady Blue River Phoenix and Shark Lady, you were 49 minutes.

You may begin your next Challenge using Stichomancy to make the Ring Materialise."

They sit on the floor. Beside each of them are two Burning Candles. The Phoenix draws four Ninarphain Water Symbols on each Corner of the Scroll and a Fountain at the Centre. The Shark Lady also draws four Transzaloreon Symbols for Water on the four Corners of her Scroll.

They both recite a Mantra. Each time they do this, A Ring partially appears on each Scroll and disappears. Inevitably the Ring Finally Materialises on the Phoenix Scroll, and she Wins the Task.

Limeade Congratulates her. "Well done, Grand Lady Blue River Phoenix, you have Won for Ninarphay." the Sceptre reappears, Light flashes, and they are transported to the Reaper Lands.

CHAPTER TEN

The Rats Ill Decision

Meanwhile, Back at the Bridge. The Phoenix and the Shark Lady are still Suspended in Mid-Air. The two Sprites are watching the Elf and talking amongst themselves. The Rat turns to the Rabbit and says,

"They are still in the same place, not moving." The Rabbit tells the Rat. Grand Lady, Blue River Phoenix, told us they're battling on the Astral Planes."

Just then, the Elf begins pulling items out of the Pot. First, a bag of nine Gold Coins pours them on the Ground.

Than a Stone Statue of a Sprite. Next, he pulls out a Black Metal Chalice, a Silver Goblet, a Nickel Watch, nine Marble Stones, a Wooden Nymph Insignia, and a priceless Platinum Jewel.

The Rat turns to the Rabbit and says. "we made it to Ninarphay. Why is the River Phoenix keeping us waiting."

The Rabbit responds saying. "you know why! She has to fight for our well-being." The Rat, with Guile and Arrogance, speaks to the Rabbit,

"I'm tired of waiting; we have all we need just across the River. Riches beyond belief, I'm going." The Rabbit tells the Rat,

"Suit yourself, but there will be Consequences." The Rat Jumps across the River and crosses over to the Elf.

The Rat then digs his Hand into the Pot and carries away Gold Coins. He walks into the Shiny Forest, but as he goes more profound, the Night draws in.

It gets darker, and his Gold Coins become Mud; when he gets to the Other Side, it is Right where he started, except the Rabbit, Shark, Phoenix, and Elf are all Statues and the Light that once was is now Darkness.

The Air is Cloudy, the water still Murky, and the Woods infested with Creatures from the Underworld Back in Transzalore.

Back in the Reaper's Realm. The Phoenix and the Shark appear in the Grand Lord Reapers Palace. They are Greeted by the Grand Lord Reaper himself. The Grand Lord Reaper says to the Phoenix.

"Grand Phoenix, your Muse sent me a Scroll of urgency saying that you are in a Pact of Challenges with the Shark Lady of Transzalore.

I understand this is your final Challenge for the Nine Fountains of Ninarphay. As this is Peaceful, I will continue my duties and explain your last Challenge.

You will both Battle for the final Ring. Whoever Wins this Ring Wins the final Fountain. The Challenge is to Fight in the Ring of Combat; three rounds begin!"

The two rivals are transported to an Arena where they are given their Respective Corners and Battle. A Buzzer sounds, and they begin to Battle.

They Fight with their Legs and Arms, Claw to Fin, Beak to Teeth. The Battle Rages on, but in the end, like with all Challenges, the Phoenix is Victorious and s Awarded the Ring.

The solid Gold Fountain sprouts Clean Water and is transported back to Ninarphay Forest, where the Rabbit is Patently waiting.

The Bridge is finally built, and the Phoenix has Conciliatory Words. "you thought well, Shark Lady of Aquarium Tower Transzalore, but as you know, the energies of Ninarphay would always Benefit a True Ninarphaian over a Transzaloreon

, and as a Grand Lady, I was always going to Win." The Shark Lady replies. "That may be true, but I would never back down as a Governess.

Farewell, Phoenix Lady of Ninarphay, You deserve all your Victory." The Shark Lady disappears into the water and is transported back to Transzalore.

The Phoenix turns to the Rabbit and says. "Where is the Rat?" The Rabbit responds by saying. "He became Greedy and crossed the River." The Phoenix

tells the Rabbit. "Then he will stay in Transzalore Forever. Come with me, Red Rabbit Sprite. You will have Riches in my Kingdom."

The Rabbit climbs onto the Back of the Phoenix, and they Fly away.

THE END.

NINARPHAY TALES VOL. III

Oni King Of Transzalore, A Love Tale

CHAPTER ONE

The Oni Kings Ultimatum

The Oni King of Transzalore sits amongst his nine Council Members in his Underworld Palace.

Arrafrayer Banshee High Priestess of Transzalore, Eroduit Wise Hermit Lord of Transzalore, Herothro Powerful Sorcerer Lord of Transzalore, Hiethreiet Sprite Queen of Transzalore, Heimlayer Oni Queen of Transzalore, Histall Ogre Priest of Transzalore, Ephream Great Elf Queen of Transzalore, Iterad Goblin Prince of Transzalore, Itamae Goblin Princess of Transzalore are all sitting around The Oni Kings high Council Chamber Table.

The ten Council Members are discussing the Politics of Transzalore and a current Noble Project they plan to implement.

The Oni King has dark coloured Clothes wearing all Black, and he also has long Plaited Hair. His Eyes are Auburn and also, and he always has a sharp, Serious Expression, although his face is round and smiley.

The Oni King has a Silver and Gold Crown on his Head. The Crown is embedded with Black Diamonds. The Rest of the Council wear mostly Black, although shades of Red and Silvery White are also Common Place on their Dress Code.

In front of them is a Hammer each for Ruling for or against Bills. At the Centre of the Table is a Magic Plinth. This Magic Plinth is used to put Bills and Orders into Effect.

The Oni King begins the meeting he says, "High Counsel of Transzalore, I welcome you here TodayToday to discuss the release of Young Children from our Realm into Ninarphay. The Rules of Today's Meeting and the use of your Hammers are, bang, the Hammer twice for yes if you agree with the Ruling and once for no if you disagree with the Meetings Ruling."

The Oni King bangs his Hammer, and the meeting commences. The Oni King continues to tell them, "Fellow Council Members, I have called you here because of a Great Concern. I believe the Realm of Transzalore is far too Cruel and Wicked for the Young to Live and stay here, and I have called the Dragon Lord of Ninarphay here to put proceedings in Place that will End this War and see the Young Promoted to their Rightful Place before the fall of Ninarphay twenty years ago. I have Summoned the Dragon Lord to take the Enslaved Ninarphay Children to the Contented Lands of Ninarphay. Has anybody got any Questions before we Rule on this Issue?"

Arrafrayer speaks, "I believe in this Just Cause, and Oni King, believe me, I am on your Side in the Northern Area of the Kingdom Realm. An Ogre Rebellion is Looming, and my Sources tell me Dark Lord Zenith of the Northern Tribes is Plotting to overthrow the Griffin Lands in Revenge for the four Crowns he Lost a Decade ago to the Grand Griffin at the Peak of the War. From what I understand, he is also planning to take over a few of your Territories, Oni King, in a bid to hold Greater Sway over Transzalore."

Oni King Turns to Histall and asks, "Histall, what do you know about this? Be Truthful, whomsoever has a Seat on my Council is a Trusted Member of the Transzalore Hierarchy."

His tall speaks; he tells the Oni King, "Dark Lord Zenith is my Leader, and I am second in Command only to him in the Northern Tribes."

Oni King retorts, ", Yes, we know that, but what is he Planning!"

His tall tells him, "he is Plotting to overthrow the Griffin Lands and take back the four Crowns, but I have not heard anything about him and an Army taking Territories from the Oni King."

Arrafrayer says, "Maybe he kept that Part of his Plan Secret because you are on the Oni Kings Counsel."

Oni King Asks, "What is your Stance on this oncoming War then, Histall?"

His tall tells the Counsel, "I tried to say to Master Zenith darkened Ogre Logic and Traditions isn't the way we should be looking at our Future and that Children deserve a better Life then Servitude, but he wouldn't listen, I keep Warning Master Zenith we should be looking at ways of Fairness and read Scriptures from the Noble Book of Ogres, but he won't listen to anyone's Counsel.

He is Hell-bent on destroying the Griffin Lands, obsessed with Past Victories and Conquests."

Oni King says, ", Well, yes, I am not bothered with Zeniths' Obsessive walk to Conquest, but be sure of one thing if he goes too far, he'll have my Uncle to answer to, and my Uncle is Seriously Powerful; what are the Opinions of everybody else?"

Hiethreiet comments, "Transzalores System of Community isn't Designed for the Young, our Systems are Based on War, Procurement of Wealth, Banditry and elated Competitiveness. I have a Heart which tells me to send the Young to Ninarphay."

Oni King states, "So it is decided we have to Vote; yes, we send the Young to Ninarphay; no, they remain in Transzalore."

They each grab their Hammers, and nine of them bang once. Herothro bangs twice. The magical Plinth displays the Votes cast on 9/1. The Oni King calls in his Counsel, Smith.

Oni King calls, "Smith, I need your assistance at once to enter the Council Chamber!"

Smith enters the Council Chambers through Giant Wooden Doors, tasselled with Iron Locks and Borders. He approaches the Counsel Table.

The Oni King tells Smith, "Smith send word to the Dragon Lord immediately; I am preparing a Scroll to release all the captured, imprisoned and Enslaved Young from Transzalore to Ninarphay with immediate Effect."

Smith retorts, ", Yes, my King."

The Oni King waves his Magical Sceptre and opens a Portal at the Centre of the Plinth. Smith climbs onto the Table and walks through the Portal.

The High Council leave the Table, and Smith arrives in Ninarphay at the Dragon Lords Grand Castle.

CHAPTER TWO

The Dragon Lord's Journey

At the Entrance to the Dragon Lords Grand Castle, there are two Statues of Dragons holding a Candelabrum.

Smith stands at the entrances beholding a Beautiful Field and a Wonderful Flower filled Scenery. Smith walks over to the Drawbridge and bangs on the Door.

A Guard exclaims, "Who goes there!"

Smith replies, "Great Goblin Smith, Loyal Consort of the Oni King of Transzalore. I have a Proposition for the Grand Dragon Lord!"

The Guard says, "You may enter!"

The Drawbridge lowers, the Doors open, and Smith enters the Castle, walking towards the Grand Dragon Lords' Throne Room.

In the Throne Room, the Dragon Lord is waiting. Smith enters the Throne Room and approaches the Dragon Lord. The Dragon Lord asks Smith, "I understand you have a Proposition for me?"

Smith responds, ", Yes, my Lord."

The Dragon Lord then asks, "What may this be?"

Smith Presents the Dragon Lord with a Scroll. The Dragon Lord then takes the Scroll from Smith and reads it.

Smith explains, "The Oni King is propositioning to release all the Young from Transzalore; he is acquiring them now and needs your approval to Grant them a safe Passage to Ninarphay."

The Dragon Lord tells Smith, "I'll prepare my things. We leave immediately."

Meanwhile, in Narnyae, the Dark Realm is just below Transzalore. Great Sorcerer Herothro is selling out the Council to the Demon King of Narnia.

Herothro tells Demon King, "The Oni King of Transzalore has gone Mad. He plans to send the Young of Transzalore to the Contented Lands."

Demon King replies, "Where is that? The Chrysalis Mountains?"

Herothro responds, ", No, my Lord, he is planning to send them to the Kingdom Realms of Ninarphay."

Demon King exclaims, "What! This is Madness anyway; it doesn't concern me. It isn't my Realm."

Herothro tells Demon King, "The Dragon Lord is on his way as we speak."

Demon King retorts, "So!"

Herothro tells him, "So a Dragons Heart can Grant Immortality if you know how to consume it."

Demon King then turns to his Guards and says, "Guards take this Sorcerer to the Dungeon Lands. We're going to Transzalore."

The Guards Cast a Spell and imprison the Sorcerer. They take Herothro to the Dungeon Lands, and Demon King opens a Portal to Transzalore.

Back with Smith and the Dragon Lord. They both enter a Portal to the Oni Kings Transzalore Castle. The Dragon Lord and Smith walk towards the Oni Kings Castles Drawbridge.

An Evil Witch from the Dystopian Slums attacks them with her Band of Conjured Shadow Monks.

The Evil Witch shouts to them, "The young of Transzalore shall remain in Transzalore."

The Shadow Monks attack like Ninjas, and the Dragon Lord and Smith fend them off.

The Grand Dragon Lord says to Smith, "Stay behind me. I can handle this Witch."

With his Claw, the Dragon Lord swings and kicks at the Shadow Monks kicking and clawing them into the distance without breaking a sweat or breathing heavily.

He then breathes Fire on the Witch. The Witch evaporates before reassembling and flying off on her Broomstick.

Smith and the Dragon Lord arrive at the Oni Kings Castle. The Dragon Lord greets the Oni King, and they begin their Summit.

The Oni King tells the Dragon Lord, "Welcome to my Realm, Dragon Lord of Ninarphay. Please make yourself Comfortable."

The Dragon Lord seats himself at the Summit Table, and discussions begin. The Dragon Lord tells the Oni King, "I am pleased you invited me here to End this War."

The Oni King retorts, "I was Persuaded by my Uncle to release the Young and stop the War but also for Personal Reasons like the Religious Ethics we hold above them is Unfair.

In Transzalore, we Award Greed and Panda Militant Attitudes, our Religious views are of War and War Gods way too Deep for Children, the Children can no longer stay in Transzalore, and as the King of this Land, I decide who can stay and go.

Some of the Regional Aristocracy hold their own Power in their own Regions, but I can still have Sway over their Decisions."

The Dragon Lord responds to the Oni King, "So I guess this means the War is Over?"

The Oni King retorts, "No, Far from it; the War has just begun. Dark Lord Zeniths Obsession with Ninarphay is out of Control, and now he and the Beast are Corrupting the Minds of the Aristocracy with Propaganda and Hollow Promises. I Fear there will soon be an Uprising, and I will be Powerless to stop it.

In Transzalore, there are only two more as Powerful as me, the Beast and Dark Lord Zenith, Dark Lord Zenith is Obsessed with the Griffin Lands and the Loss of his Enslaved four Crowns".

The Dragon Lord asks, "So where are the Children?"

The Oni King tells him, "They have all been gathered in my Castle and given Lessons of the Love and Contentedness that await them in Ninarphay.

Whenever you are ready, we can begin rounding them up. I will use my Sceptre to open the Portal and let them through."

Demon King arrives in the Oni Kings Court through the Portal and searches for the Dragon Lord.

He approaches the Castle, but a Spy is on Hand waiting for him as he enters. She says, "I am the Dystopian Witch and Grand Merchant of the Oni King."

Demon King replies, "Are you the Witch Spy I was told about?"

The Witch responds, ", Yes, I am, and I shall show you the shortcut to the Oni King's main Palace."

She pushes on a Wall Panel, and a Secret Passageway opens up. She tells him, "my Family built this Castle but was then sent to Govern the Slums when the Oni King was selected for Power!"

Demon King asks, "Why did he do that?"

The Witch answers, "It came to light that I was stealing Important Information that could have overthrown the Oni Kings Rule."

Demon King asks, "And was you?"

The Witch answers, "The Oni King was too Nice; he made Decisions that led to Harmony and the Regents before he had Valued Procuring Wealth, Strengthening Militia, exploring Decadence, and only Caring about ourselves; that's why I did it; we're here now."

The Witch presses her Ear on an Air Vent and hears them talking. She says, "I can Hear them talking. The Dragons Heart is yours for the taking. Get your Blade ready!"

Demon King draws his Blade and prepares to pounce. The Dystopian Witch tells him, "On my mark, I will push the Panel in 4,3,2,1!" She pushes the Panel, and Demon King jumps from behind the wall plunging his Blade into the Dragon's Chest.

He makes the incision, and the dragon's Heart is soon beating in his Palm. Oni King shouts, "Demon King from the Realm of Narnyae, what are you doing here?"

Demon King retorts, "I am stealing a Heart to become Immortal, my Dear Oni King!" The Oni King shouts to his Guards, "Guards seize him!" The Witch bursts in just as she and Demon King Look are surrounded. She drops a Bile on the floor, inciting a dispersal Spell Mantra.

"Source of light, darkness and Spite take us from this Place of fright!" They disappear, and The Oni King goes to the Dragon Lord and apologises.

"Grand Dragon Lord, I am profoundly sorry. I never knew this would happen."

CHAPTER THREE

Demon Kings Cruelty

The Dragon Lord tells him, "It's Fine. I knew when I came here it would be Dangerous!" The Dragon Lord's Talon turns to Stone. The Oni King tells him, "I'll get your Heart back for you!"

He exits his Castle to pursue the Demon King, grabbing the Dragon Lord's Sceptre. The Oni King follows the two Thieves through the Narnyae Portal.

Demon King of Narnyae and his Aide, the Slum Witch, arrive in Narnyae. The Oni King arrives in Narnyae, but because of the Temporal Disturbance of the Dragon Lord's Sceptre, he arrives on the other side of the Realm.

The Oni King has arrived at Shangri-La's Citadel 100 kilometres from Demon Kings Empire. Demon King turns to the Witch and says, "Where are we?" The Witch replies, "We are in Narnyae, the Hell Realm, not too far from your Palace."

Demon King replies, "your wrong. We are just on the border. My Palace is about ten-kilo meters from here." All of a Sudden, a Giant Centaur approaches them and says, "You are in Shangrilas Slave House. You must work!"

Demon King responds, "Do you know who I am? I am Demon King of Narnyae, your Lord and Master. I will not bow to anybody in this Place."

The Centaur responds, "I don't care who you are; I only serve Shangri-La. You will Work!" Standing around 30 feet tall, the Giant Centaur slams his Hammer at Demon King, and the two begin fighting.

Demon King is soon Successful, and the Centaur says, "You are Truly a Devil Lord of Narnyae!" The Centaur then passes out.

Demon King then signals his flying Chariot to pick him up at Shangri-La's Citadel. The Chariot arrives, the Slum Witch and Demon King board the Chariot, and they fly away.

Oni King arrives in Shangri-La's Slave House. The Slave House is ten-kilo metres Long, and the thousands of Slave girls that occupy it live in appalling Conditions.

The Portal closes. The Event is witnessed by twelve Giant Centaurs. The Oni King enters his Eight Trigram Crow Stance and begins to Battle the twelve Centaurs.

Eight fall almost instantly, and the next four fall even quicker. They all get up and stand in a twelve-Point Circle. They Conjure a Barrier Spell that lasts long enough for them to get close.

The Oni King soon breaks the Barrier Spell and says, "Let's wrap this up then, shall we!" He stamps his foot towards the floor, and the shock waves cause the Walls to tumble Down. He enters his Sixteen-Point Trigram Stance and begins to Battle, knocking them out completely.

More Giant Centaurs come running. He stamps his foot into a Thirty-Two-Point Trigram, taking out the first wave, then Sixty-Four-Point Trigram taking out the second wave, and finally, a One Hundred And Twenty-Eight-Point Trigram levelling out the final wave.

The ones that are not entirely Unconscious attempt to leave, and the Oni King lets them. He begins to explore the Slave House walking through the Rubble until he comes to a Part of the Slave House that is Undamaged.

A Slave girl runs up to him and thanks him. She says, "Thank you for saving me, great Lord!" Oni King replies, "Why are you thanking me? I was just doing my duty." The Slave girl tells him, "Just as you came, I was due to be Executed."

The Oni King asks, "Why were they going to Execute you?" The Slave girl replies, "Queen Shangri-La wants me to Worship her and to keep me as a Muse, but it is against my Faith. I have an Amulet that warns me to stay Faithful and Virtuous, Worshipping only Goodness and Grace. It was magically Tattooed on my Skin by my Parents, the ones I've never known ever since I was a Baby. You see, I was Orphaned here as a Baby and never knew my Family." The Oni King waves the Sceptre over her, and an Image appears of Centaurs riding away with her as a Baby through a Portal.

Oni King tells her, "The Sceptre showed me Centaurs riding away with you, but it is Blocked up to that point and won't show me any more.

It must be Great Magic Guarding you to repel such a Powerful Sceptre. Come with me; I'll Protect you." The Slave girl says, "My name is Dolores. I am a Sprite."

Oni King replies, "I am the Oni King of Transzalore. I will keep your Safe Journey with me."

Demon King is flying to his Palace over the Mountains of Shangri-La's City, meanwhile, in his Palace. Nafrayer Demon Kings Goblin Servant is making Preparations for his arrival.

She stands in the Palace Tower and, through Binoculars, views his approach. She walks down the Stairs to the Main Hall and tells her Servants, "Prepare for the King's arrival. He will be here soon, so prepare a Banquet and ensure the Palace is Clean and Tidy."

The Oni King and Dolores continue walking through Shangri-La's Citadel. Dolores walks behind The Oni King, trying to keep up with his pace. The Oni King turns and says to her, "Climb on my back if you can't keep up!"

She does so, and they keep on walking. More Centaurs soon come; they are bigger and stronger than the last. The Oni says to Dolores, "Go and hide somewhere Safe!"

He continues to Battle them, and they are soon Defeated. The Oni King Signals to Dolores to approach him. She does so and asks, "What are we going to do now?"

The Oni King tells her, "You're going to tell me where the Masters are hiding, then we're going to find them and Conquer them, then we're going to Wonder into Demon Kings Palace."

Dolores tells him, "Their Main Lair is on the border of the Citadel and the Demon Kings Palace. I know where it is; I can take you there". The Oni King says, ", Well, let's go then!"

They continue their Arduous search for the Boarder, and an hour later, they reach it. The border is Guarded by hundreds of Centaurs.

Dolores turns to the Oni King and asks, "Are you really going to Defeat all of them?" The Oni King responds to her question, saying, "With ease!"

The Oni King Wonders through the Citadel, Freeing hundreds of Slaves. He tells them, "Today, you have Earned your Freedom. Go forth and Banish ways of Sin and Malice for Virtue!"

The Slaves Cheer and go forth. The Oni King turns to Dolores and asks, "Do you know any Secret Routes to Demon Kings Palace?" Dolores tells him,

"across the border, we built an Underground Tunnel during the Rebellion. I can take you to the Heart of the Palace without anyone ever knowing."

They Cross the Border and walk towards the Palace. Dolores takes the Oni King through a Cove Underlay that leads to a Cave that leads to a Tunnel, which leads to the Palace.

They walk through the Cave until they get to a Secret Passageway that leads to an Underground Tunnel, where they continue their Journey.

Demon King flies Overhead towards his Palace. He enters his Realm. He Lands on his Tower and is Greeted by his Goblin Servant, Nafrayer.

Nafrayer says, "Welcome back to the Realm, my King. The Servants have prepared you a Banquet." With the Dragon Lord.s beating Heart in his hand, he says, "After this, we will have to find a Sorcerer to Liquefy his Heart and make it Edible."

They walk to the Banquet Area of Demon Kings Palace; Nafrayer and the Dystopian Witch sit down at the Banquet and begin to feast.

CHAPTER FOUR

The Oni Kings

GOOD DEED

Nafrayer sneaks off to her Bedroom, where she opens a Secret Underground Door to a Tunnel, sits at her Shrine, and says a Prayer.

"O god of Holy Light and Virtue, give me the Love, Will and Faith to do what's Right through my Trials and Hardship."

She then lights a Candle, Places a Ruby, a Prayer Sheet and Ash Over the Fire. Dolores and the Oni King fast approach Nafrayer holding the Dragon Lord's Sceptre.

The Oni King sees Nafrayer blowing out the Candle Fire by the Shrine. He waves the Sceptre, which shows Nafrayer praying by the Candlelight with Virtue.

The Oni King approaches her and asks her for help, "Excuse me, kind Goblin I saw you praying and would like to know who is this Graceful God you are praying to."

Nafrayer responds, "I am praying to the God of Love and Glory." The Oni King asks, "If you are praying to such a Good and Gracious God, why are you living in Narnyae?"

Nafrayer tells him, "I was Born to this Realm, but one day, I was visiting Shangri-La's Citadel, where a Slave girl was being Tortured into Submission by Shangri-La herself. When they had stopped, they sent me to Cleanse her. I touched her Scarred Arm, trying to Clean what I Thought was a Wound but was actually a Tattoo, and then fell into a Violent Fever. I had a Vision; I began having Dreams when I returned to the Palace. Since then, I've been worshipping Devoutly."

Oni King pulls Dolores from the Shadows and says, "Was this the girl?" Nafrayer says, ", Yes, this is the girl!"

The Oni King then tells her, "I am the Awe Powerful Oni King of Transzalore, and I need your help to thwart Demon King and return something. Dear, for your Reward, I will Grant you a Place in Transzalore as my Aide," Nafrayer grabs his Arm and says, "Follow me. I know a Secret Route into the Grand Hall."

They walk through the Tunnel and ascend the Stairs into Nafrayers Chamber.

Demon King finishes his Banquet at the Food Court. His Servants immediately Rush Over and Clean him. He calls over his Magi Consort.

"High Lord Magi, we need to Liquefy this Heart immediately so I can Consume it and become Immortal." His High Lord Magi walks towards him and says, "My King, no one in this Kingdom is Powerful enough to Evoke such a Spell; no one has expertise in this Field. The only one who Possesses such a Skill is Herothro, who is Locked in the Dungeons." With Great Anger and Guile, Demon King exclaims, ", Well, Summon him at once!"

Meanwhile, The Oni King walks down the Hallway holding the Dragon Lord's Sceptre. The Oni King, Delores and Nafrayer enter the Food Court Balcony through a Secret Panel.

The Oni King stands at the Top of the Balcony holding the Dragon Lord's Sceptre, staring at Demon King. He witnesses Demon King holding the Dragon Lord's Heart in his Hand.

The Oni King Whispers to Nafrayer, "Keep Dolores Safe and wait here." He jumps from the Balcony onto the Centre of the Court. "Demon King, as Oni King of Transzalore, I cannot allow you to Steal from a Comrade and Fellow Steward. Return what you have Stolen immediately!"

The Oni King waves the Sceptre, and the Heart appears in the Centre of the Sceptre. Demon King Screams, "Never!" A Battle breaks out, and Demon King is soon Defeated after a Battle of Brawn, Wits and Magic.

The Oni King stands over Demon King and says, "You are not Strong enough to Defeat me. Besides, I out Rank you; get Stronger!"

The Oni King Signals to Nafrayer and Dolores, and they jump from the Balcony. The Oni King waves the Sceptre, and a Portal opens. They step into the Portal, and moments Later, they are Back in Transzalore.

They arrive at the Castle and enter the Summit Room. The Dragon Lord's Body is Half Stone. Oni King says, "Grand Dragon Lord, I have returned with your Heart."

The Dragon Lord doesn't respond, but his eyes move. Nafrayer says, "Give his Heart to me. I never told Demon King this, but I know Dragonology." Nafrayer takes the Heart, Places it in the Dragon Lord's Body, and the Dragon Lord soon Heals.

The Dragon Lord makes a Full Recovery. The Young of Transzalore is sent to Ninarphay through five Grand Portals held open by the Grand Griffin, The Grand Blue River Phoenix, The Grand Dragon Lord, Queen Bear and The Oni King.

The Portals close and Seal. The Oni King sits on his Throne with Dolores as his Favoured and Nafrayer as his Aide. He turns and says to them, "We must find out which Realm you belong to, Dolores.

THE END

NINARPHAY TALES VOL. IV

Queen Bear And The Nine Ninarphay Talismans

CHAPTER ONE

Preservation Of The Young

The Dragon Lord flies into his Castle, rests his Sceptre in front of him on his Grand Stool, and sits back in his Throne Chair. He sighs in relief and then says to his Aide, Great Countess Levy. "My Beloved Fairy."

Great Countess Levy approaches his Throne and says, ", Yes, my Lord." He replies, "I need you to do something for me." She responds, "What might that be, my Lord."

He tells her, "You must call a Summit of the Nine Grand Lords of Ninarphay. I would have done it before I left, but it was too Short Notice." Levy asks, "So I take it your Journey was a Success!"

The Dragon Lord tells her, "It was, but it almost turned very Sour very quickly. When I arrived, most of the Transzaloreons were very accommodating, then a Narnyae Devil appeared and Stole my Heart."

Levy is unnerved. She replies with a look of Fear, "O' my, how did you ever Survive?" The Dragon Lord clutches his Chest and says, "Through the Noble and Sound actions of the Oni King, of course!

He chased the Narnyae Devil through Narnyae, Reclaimed my Heart and set the Young Free as Promised." Levy looks out of the Window and sees thousands of Children arriving through Portals.

Levy says, "So I guess the Mission was a Success; thank you for the Council; I will call the Eight Ninarphay Grand Lords at once." She walks towards her Council Chamber and picks up her Wand. She uses an Incantation to Message the other Grand Lords.

A telly display appears, and the Eight Grand Lords can be seen in them. She tells them, "Grand Lords of Ninarphay, today we have Won a Great Victory, and the Young have been Freed from Transzalore.

You are needed at the Grand Dragon Lords Castle immediately; please bring your whole Counsel."

They all agree to be there immediately. The Grand Griffin, The Queen Bear and the Blue River Phoenix are already there with their Consort. Soon all of the Grand Lords arrive in the Dragon Lords Castle.

The Nine Ninarphay Lords sit at the Dragon Lords Summit Table, and the Dragon Lord speaks. The Dragon Lord tells them, "As we speak, thousands of Ninarphay Children are being taken to Safekeeping by my Courtiers across the Kingdom."

The Grand Griffin speaks, "There are plans for each of them as laid out on the Ninarphay Scrolls." Grand Turtle says, "On the Ninarphay Scrolls, it states each Child shall be appointed Housing, Education and Training."

Queen Tiger then speaks, "No doubt we are holding this Summit to Cement the Guidelines laid out in the Scrolls." The Dragon Lord tells them, "That is why I called you all here today.

After my Journey to Transzalore, the Noble Oni King set Free all of the Young as a Jest of Good Faith. When a Narnyaen showed up and Stole my Heart, he moved Mountains to Retrieve it and held Strong to his Promise."

The Grand Reaper says, ", Well, that is my Nephew, so how are we going to do this?" The Dragon Lord tells them, "The designated Children each have a Destiny path in Ninarphay.

Lords, you will each Escort one-ninth of the Children to your Lands where they will each have a Home, Education and Training as well as Specific Care Special to each of your Lands."

The Queen Bear talks, "Grand Lords, me and the Great Fairy Esmeral have uncovered Plans to Steal the nine Ninarphay Talismans being kept in my Kingdom."

Queen Witch says, "So what do you suggest?" Queen Bear tells her, "I suggest each of you take your Respective Talismans and hold them in your Respective Castles."

The Grand Tengu asks, "Did you bring them here?" Queen Bear tells them, "It was to Short Notice I was called to help with the Sceptre Portals and had no time to retrieve them."

The Grand Reaper asks, "What else do you know of this Plot?" Queen Bear tells them, "The two Lords who Plan to Acquire them are in the Top five Power Bracket of Transzalore; one is second, the other is fifth.

The Beast of Transzalore and Dark Lord Nobi, I also found that they want to overthrow us and take our Kingdom Lands." The Dragon Lord tells them, "First things first, we Enrol and Safeguard the Children. Then Queen Bear and Great Fairy Esmeral will deal with the Talismans.

Everybody ready to go?" They all let out a Great Cheer in Unison. They leave the Table, gather their Respective Children then lead them to their Respective Lands.

CHAPTER TWO

The Envy Of Dark Lords

Meanwhile, in the Beast of Transzalores Lair in Transzalore. The Beast of Transzalore Hog and his Nefarious Partner in Crime, Dark Lord Nobi, are hatching a Plot to overthrow Ninarphay.

Dark Lord Nobi stands over Hog in Hogs Castle Lair. Hog sits on his dark Lord Throne, and the two dark Lords discuss taking the nine Ninarphay Talismans.

Hog tells Dark Lord Nobi, "Us combining Forces to bring down the nine Kingdoms of Ninarphay is Genius." Dark Lord Nobi responds, "As two of the most Powerful Beings in Transzalore, the nine Grand Lords have no chance whatsoever.

We'll hit them before they've even realised it. If only we had more Allies backing us, Victory would be Assured." Hog says to Nobi, "what do you mean Assured? Victory is Assured already."

Dark Lord Nobi corrects himself, "What I meant was we should have the Oni King on our side." Hog tells him, "It's because of Oni's Good Deeds to Ninarphay why I am doing this anyway.

We must uphold Transzalores dark name and rectify our Status as the dark World by stealing the Talismans. We will show the Grand Lords and Ninarphay that we are Cruel and Mean."

A Goblin walks in and tells the Pair, "Master Hog, Dark Lord Nobi, the Portal is ready. It had a Major Block, but the Guardian Dalu guarding it has a Transzaloreon Nature."

Hog says out Loud, "Perfect!" The two Dark Lords then walk through the Portal and are Greeted by the Guardian Dalu, an Elf Guardian. Dalu exclaims to them, "Halt! Who goes there?"

Dark Lord Nobi conjures a glowing Golden Jewel, takes it to him, and says, "Dalu, I am Dark Lord Nobi of Transzalore, and I am here to make an Ultimatum with you."

Dalu responds strongly, saying, "What could you possibly give me that I have not already got?" Dalu explains, "Riches, your own Land in Transzalore, a Lordship and Freedom to do whatever you want whenever you want."

Dalu lowers his guard, "And what must I do to achieve this?" Hog exclaims, "Give us the nine Ninarphay Talismans and come with us to Transzalore, where you will Rule as a High Courtier!"

Dalu opens the Vault, retrieves the nine Ninarphay Talismans, and Hands them to Dark Lord Nobi. He then says, "I accept your offer." Nobi says, "Come with us. We could use your Skills in Transzalore." The three Transzaloreons leave the Vault open and cross the Portal to Transzalore.

The Queen Bear, Great Fairy Esmeral and their Consort arrive in the Queen Bears Kingdom with thousands of Ninarphaian Children. Queen Bear sees to it that the Children are Ordered and Cared for.

After she arranges for the Children to be Housed and Cared for appropriately, The Queen Bear and Great Fairy Esmeral attend the Vault. Once they arrive, they are shocked by what they see.

Queen Bear stands at the Entrance to the Vault, turns to Esmeral, and says, "Great Fairy Esmeral, I cannot believe the State of this Place! Where is the Elf Guardian Dalu?

He may have disappeared with the Loot and possibly those two Dark Lords. Esmeral, wave your Wand and let us see what Events took Place here!"

Esmeral waves her Wand and Chants an Incantation. "Reveal!" A golden glow is displayed in the room, revealing Dalu talking to Hog and Dark Lord Nobi.

It then displays him excepting a Jewel. Soon after, it shows them stealing the Talismans and Dalu, leaving with them through the Portal. Queen Bear turns to Esmeral, saying, "They have the Talismans!"

Great Fairy Esmeral responds by saying, "We are too late. They took the Jewels, and one of our best Guardians has defected. What are we going to do?"

Queen Bear reaches for her Sceptre, grips it tightly in her hand, and says to Great Fairy Esmeral, "Esmeral, we must go on a Mission to Transzalore."

Esmeral responds to Queen Bear, saying, "But Transzalore is Dangerous. We'll need Reinforcements." Queen Bear tells her, "Esmeral, this is no time for Cowardice. You must have Faith.

We must go to Transzalore to Retrieve the nine Talismans. We must Retrieve the Talismans before they are put to use."

Esmeral says, "If it is my Queen's Righteous Wisdom, I will Regard her True and Powerful Words!"

Queen Bear says, "We leave at once." The Queen Bear slices the Sceptre through the Air, and the two Ninarphaians instantly Travel to Transzalore. They begin their search for Guardian Dalu, Dark Lord Nobi and the Beast of Transzalore Hog.

They arrive in Labyrinth Castle Hogs Lair. Queen Bear turns to Esmeral and says, "Esmeral, have your Enchanted Wand guide us to where Nobi, Dalu and Hog are Lurking."

Esmeral says, "Right away, my Queen!" Esmeral waves her Wand, and the Wand lays out a Map to lead them to where the Nefarious Creatures are Lurking.

Esmeral tells Queen Bear, "All we have to do is follow the Wand." Queen Bear says, "Let's go then!" Hog, Nobi and Dalu open a Portal. Hog tells them, "We have the nine Talismans. It is Time for Phase Two of our Plan."

Nobi says, "We Enslave Ninarphay! Dalu, are you with us?" Dalu tells them, "to Live like a Grand Lord and have everything I want. Hell yeah. Let's go!"

Search For The Nine Talks

They walk through the Portal, and Queen Bear and Esmeral arrive as they leave. The Portal begins closing, and Esmeral and Queen Bear chase the Portal, but it closes.

Queen Bear tries to reopen the Portal but is wholly locked off. Esmeral asks, "What do we do now, Queen Bear?" Queen Bear tells her, "We must combine forces, my Sceptre and your Wand.

We must find them and stop them before it's too late. When they make it to Ninarphay, they could Enslave the entire Realm with those Talismans!" Esmeral says, "then what are we waiting for!" Esmeral holds up her Wand and says, "Hurry up!"

Queen Bear incites a Mantra. "Esmeral, use your Wand to track their Location. I'll open a Portal." Esmeral tracks their Location, and Queen Bear uses her Sceptre to open a Portal, which only partially opens.

Queen Bear says, "This will take a while."

CHAPTER FOUR

Enslaved Pantheon Lord

Meanwhile, in the Griffin Lands, it is Night, and everyone is asleep. The Portal opens in the Grand Griffins Bed Chamber, and he is fast asleep all alone.

The three Nefarious Creatures sneak up on him and place the Talisman around his neck. They then use the Talismans and Sceptre to open a Portal to the Phoenix Lands.

Esmeral and Queen Bear finally break through the Portal and arrive at the Grand Griffins Sky Castle. They awake the Grand Griffin from his slumber and notice his eyes are glazed over.

He is controlled by the Talisman. They try to remove it, but it is impossible. The Talisman is attached to his neck and cannot be removed.

They keep attempting to remove it, but as it loosens slightly, the Talisman's Power blasts them away, and they hit the Wall. Queen Bear turns to Esmeral and says, "Esmeral, conjure a binding Chain we need to subdue him."

Esmeral responds, "Right away, my Queen!" Esmeral uses her Wand to conjure a Magical binding Chain. The Chain appears, and Queen Bear and Esmeral use it to bind the Grand Griffin.

Queen Bear tells Esmeral, "Chances are the Evil trio are at the Phoenix Lands." Esmeral asks, "What do we do, Queen Bear?" Queen Bear tells her, "We must see my counterpart, Queen Tiger.

From there, she will know what to do. Let's go!" The Queen Bear Incites a Mantra waves her Sceptre, and a Portal opens to the Tiger Lands.

CHAPTER FIVE

The Desperate Plight Of The Pheonix

Meanwhile, in the Grand Phoenix's Castle. The Grand Phoenix is bathing in her Spring Pond. The Evil Trio Lurk inside her Castle out of sight, looking at the Grand Phoenix.

The Grand Phoenix finishes her Bath and retreats to her Slumber Chamber. She rests in her Bed, and as she is about to fall gently off to sleep, the trio ambush her and Places the Talisman around her neck. She falls unconscious, and the Evil Trio continue their Journey.

Nobi receives a Transmission from his Sceptre telling him a Portal has been opened to the Tiger Lands. He discusses it with Hog and Dalu. "Lord Hog, two beings of considerable Power have entered the Tiger Lands."

Hog responds, "Can we still go there?" Nobi tells him, "My Lord, they have entered the same place we're going to." Hog says, "We best leave it, then I suggest we see Lord Tengu."

The Evil Trio open a Portal and travel to the Tengu Lands. Esmeral and Queen Bear find Queen Tiger dining in her Luxurious Food Hall. They approach her, and Queen Tiger says,

"Queen Bear Great Fairy Esmeral, what do I owe this Honour?" Queen Bear tells her, "Queen Tiger, you must come with us immediately. You are in Great Danger!"

Queen Tiger responds, "This is about the Talismans, isn't it?" Esmeral says, ", Yes, it is!" Queen Bear tells Queen Tiger, "We must leave at once."

CHAPTER SIX

Final Battle At Lord Tengus Dojo

Hog, Nobi and Dalu arrive at the Grand Tengus Castle. Dalu turns to Hog and says, "Master, once we have captured the Grand Tengu, we will have enslaved one-third of the Grand Pantheon."

Nobi turns to Dalu and says, "We would have done that already if Queen Tiger never had escaped." Hog tells them, "You two be quiet. We still have to infiltrate and move through this Castle."

The trio hold their silence and use the Sceptre to take them to the most secluded part of the Castle closest to the Grand Tengu. They enter his Spa House, and the Spa House is completely deserted.

The Grand Tengu is in his Dojo training in unique martial art forms. He finishes training, turns off the dojo Lights and rests in his Hot Spring in his Spa House.

Hog, Nobi and Dalu are waiting and quietly hiding near the Grand Tengu, resting in his Hot Spring. They watch for a change in the Grand Tengus' activity.

Not realising he is being watched, the Grand Tengu relaxes further in the Hot Spring. The Grand Tengu sighs and closes his eyes almost as if asleep.

Nobi reaches for the Talisman and slowly extends his arm towards the Grand Tengus Neck. As the Talisman draws closer, the Grand Tengu realises what will happen.

Without delay, The Grand Tengu snatches the Talisman out of Nobi's Hand and exclaims, "What are you doing here, and how did you get in! Speak at once!"

Dalu utters repulsively, "We are Lords of Transzalore and do not answer to you!" Grand Tengu tells them, "I am Grand Tengu, Lord of Ninarphays Grand Pantheon. My combat skills are marked as the most awesome, and no Beast of Transzalore and Dark Lord Nobi with their lackey, who I've never even heard of, is defeating me here tonight."

Hog tells him, "Grand Lord Tengu, you are outnumbered, and with that outmatched, surrender now, and I will not harm you!" Grand Tengu responds, "Yes, but you are in Ninarphay and came to fight with me. Surrender now, and I will harm you."

They all then begin a battle of desperation. Dalu attempts to retrieve the Talisman from the Grand Lord Tengu, but he is sent hurtling to the Ground and is injured.

Dark Lord Nobi tries much the same, but the Grand Lord Tengus Hands are too quick, and Dark Lord Nobi is sent spinning. Hog is more Successful in grabbing the Talisman, but Grand Lord Tengu plies it away from him.

Grand Lord Tengu battles Hog and Nobi for ten minutes, getting the best of them each time until he is overpowered by the numbers game and gets sent to the Ground, clutching onto the Talisman tightly.

Dalu, in distress, reaches for the Talisman whilst on the Ground close to the grounded Lord Tengu. Hog and Nobi close in to end the battle, but Queen Tiger, Queen Bear and Esmeral soon arrive.

Grand Tengu, Queen Bear, Queen Tiger and Esmeral all begin to battle Hog, Dark Lord Nobi and Dalu. They fight long and hard, and before too long, the Power of four high-powered Ninarphaians gets the better of the Transzaloreons.

Esmeral subdues and further injures Dalu; Queen Tiger floors Nobi resting her Foot upon him, and Queen Tiger Queen Bear wrestles Hog to the Ground, holding him in a submission lock.

Nobi wrestles loose, grabs Hogs Sceptre, and summons the enslaved Grand Ninarphaians. Nobi says, "Portal far across the Lands summons the ones who for Transzalore stands!"

The Portal opens, and slowly, the Grand Griffin and the Grand Blue River Phoenix walk through the Portal one after the other. The Grand Griffin asks, "What must I do, Hog Beast of Transzalore!"

The room goes still as everybody looks at the Grand Griffin. A moment of suspense is in the Air, and everyone appears tense. Then suddenly, the Grand Griffin roars and, with his mighty Talon, strikes at Queen Bear.

The Queen Bear, hurt by the Grand Griffin's immense power, hurtles through the Air, releasing Hog from her clutches. Queen Bear is slumped out in the Corner, stunned and dazed.

Hog gets up to his feet, clutching his Arm and his Leg. He says to the Grand Griffin and the Grand Blue River Phoenix,

"I command you to attack the Grand Lords of Ninarphay without mercy!" Hog then exclaims, "Get them now!"

The Grand Blue River Phoenix and the Grand Griffin rush into battle. The Grand Blue River Phoenix attacks the Grand Tengu, who is already slightly injured. She hits him with a revolving Phoenix fist, and he uses a revolving Ravens guard to block it.

Three strikes and three guards are hit with immense power. The Phoenix hits so hard that a wind rush permeates from the Grand Tengu's guard. The Grand Griffin charges into Queen Tiger with a Griffin kick.

Queen Tiger blocks it with her tiger claw, scratching the Grand Griffin's leg deeply. She slides back from the Griffin Kick whilst maintaining her tiger claw guard stance.

Queen Tiger says to Grand Tengu, "Counter their attacks. They are not bilaterally sensible. You can injure them!"

Grand Tengu responds, "That's easy to say you're not fighting the Phoenix Lady!" Queen Tiger responds, "Oh yes, she is the best at countering. Then move bilaterally they can only follow simple Logic."

Grand Tengu exclaims, "Got it!" The Grand Tengu spins and does a moon kick. The kick connects with the Grand Blue River Phoenix, and she turns into the Wall.

The Grand Blue River Phoenix lays on the Floor for about a second, then gets back up. The Grand Tengu tells Queen Tiger, "They don't seem to be registering any Pain."

The Queen Tiger tells him, "It's the Magic of the Talismans!" Queen Bear finally gets up, holding and shaking her Head.

She charges at the Grand Griffin. Queen Bear grabs the Grand Griffin and puts him into a pile driver.

The Grand Griffin gets back up straight away. He gathers Ki in his Talons and strikes a mighty talon strike at Queen Tiger and Queen Bear. They both fall to the Ground, injured and stunned.

The Grand Blue River Phoenix knocks the Grand Tengu to the Ground, who lays on the Floor injured. Dark Lord Nobi prepares the Talismans to approach the injured and floored Grand Tengu, Queen Bear and Queen Tiger.

Just then, a Portal opens, and four Ninarphaians each rush through. The Grand Dragon Lord, Grand Lord Reaper, Queen Witch and Grand Blue Turtle each arrive.

The Grand Dragon Lord rushes over to Dark Lord Nobi, grabs the Talismans, hands them to Esmeral, and says, "Keep these safe, Esmeral!" Grand Blue Turtle rolls his shell over Hog, and Dalu is locked in a barrier spell by The Queen Witch.

Queen Witch, The Grand Reaper Attack Blue River Phoenix, The Grand Dragon Lord, and The Grand Blue Turtle attack the Grand Griffin. They are soon subdued, and they retrieve the Talismans from them.

The Grand Blue River Phoenix and the Grand Griffin return to normal, claiming they can't remember what happened. Hog, Dalu and Nobi are imprisoned in the Queen Bears Vortex Jail, and each of the Grand Lords is charged with looking after their Talismans.

THE END

Printed in the United States
by Baker & Taylor Publisher Services